THE
GIANT
SEA SERPENT

and

The Unicorn

Retold by MARGARET MAYO
Illustrated by PETER BAILEY

ORCHARD BOOKS

For Natalie
M.M.
With love to the two young whippersnappers,
Oscar and Felix
P.B.

Orchard Books
96 Leonard Street, London EC2A 4XD
Orchard Books Australia
32/45-51 Huntley Street, Alexandria, NSW 2015
The text was first published in Great Britain in the form
of a gift collection called *The Orchard Book of Magical Tales*
and *The Orchard Book of Mythical Birds and Beasts*
illustrated by Jane Ray, in 1993 and 1996
This edition first published in hardback in 2003
First paperback publication in 2004
The Orchard Book of Magical Tales Text © Margaret Mayo 1993
The Orchard Book of Mythical Birds and Beasts Text © Margaret Mayo 1996
Illustrations © Peter Bailey 2003
The rights of Margaret Mayo to be identified as the author
and Peter Bailey to be identified as the illustrator of this work
have been asserted by them in accordance with the
Copyright, Designs and Patents Act, 1988.
A CIP catalogue record for this book is available from the British Library
ISBN 1 84362 081 2 (hardback)
ISBN 1 84362 089 8 (paperback)
1 3 5 7 9 10 8 6 4 2 (hardback)
1 3 5 7 9 10 8 6 4 2 (paperback)
Printed in Great Britain

CONTENTS

THE
GIANT
SEA SERPENT

Jamie lived on a farm, not far from the sea, with his mother, father and six brothers. And because he was the youngest and smallest, everyone called him Little Jamie and made him do the boring work no one else would do, like looking after the geese!

One day, news reached the farm
that the biggest, first and father of sea
serpents, Master Stoorworm, had come
swimming from the depths of the ocean
and parked himself, head to shore and tail
to sea, at the next bay along the coast.

Master Stoorworm was immense.
His head stuck out of the sea, big as a
mountain, his two eyes were like round
shiny lakes, while his body was so long
that, stretched out, it could have reached
across the Atlantic Ocean. Right from
Europe to the shores of North America.

The monster's appetite was enormous. But he only ate breakfast. As soon as the morning sun touched his eyes, he opened his wide mouth and yawned. *"Ahhhhhh…"* he sucked in fresh air, and *"Hooooo…"* he blasted out his vile breath. It smelt like rotten fish. It was a deadly sort of smell.

Six times Master Stoorworm yawned. The seventh time he opened his mouth,

he flicked out his long and stretchy forked tongue, scooped up an enormous breakfast and flung it into his mouth. This tongue was so powerful it could knock down a house and grab the people inside. It could sweep up half a dozen cows or a boat full of fishermen. But what frightened people most was that the tongue was so long it was not possible to guess where the monster would strike next.

When Jamie's mother heard about Master Stoorworm she said, "Something must be done!"

"Someone," said his father, "will have to kill him!"

"I'd fight him," said Jamie, who was toasting his toes by the fire. "I'm not scared."

His six brothers laughed out loud and started to tease. "Little Jamie!" they shouted. "Our little brother! The *big hero*!"

Now King Harald, the ruler of that country, was an old man. But he still had a wise head on his shoulders and so he called a meeting  of The Thing, which was a council of men who met to make laws and govern. And the king told them that a brave champion must be found to kill Master Stoorworm. Then there was a babble of voices.

"He can't be killed!" said one. "Waste of time trying!"

"Somehow we've got to keep him happy!" said another.

"We could feed him tasty morsels," said a third. "Seven lovely maidens, tied up on the rocks every morning...or maybe a princess. Then the monster would leave the rest of us in peace."

"Wait!" said the king. "Wait seven more days. A champion may be found. And if he does kill Master Stoorworm, he can marry my only child, Princess Gem-de-Lovely, and inherit my kingdom. He shall also have my precious sword, Sicker Snapper, which was given to me by the god Odin himself."

News of the king's prize – a princess, a kingdom and a sword – spread throughout the kingdom and to all the lands about. And so, seven days later, about midday, a large crowd gathered by the seashore. Jamie and his family were there, alongside the king, his lovely daughter, all the members of The Thing, and *thirty-six* tough-looking champion fighters.

Some of the champions had plans, and some had not the least idea what they were going to do. But they all swaggered about looking brave until...Master Stoorworm opened his mouth and yawned a sleepy, after-breakfast yawn.

Whew! The smell of his breath was vile. Twelve champions fainted on the spot, twelve were sick and the last twelve clamped their fingers on their noses and ran.

"I see there are no champions left!"
said King Harald. "So, tomorrow, before
Master Stoorworm wakes, I shall come
myself and fight him."

"You are too old, my lord,"
said his chief steward.
"Your fighting
days are over."
The king drew out
his precious sword,
Sicker Snapper. "With
thumbs crossed on my good
sword, I tell you all," he said, "I will die
myself before my daughter or any other
maiden is offered to the monster." And he
turned to his chief steward and said,
"Prepare a boat with two stout oars, mast
up and sail ready to hoist, and order the
boatman to guard it till I come tomorrow,
before sunrise."

On their way home Jamie said to his brothers, "I'd fight Master Stoorworm. Really I would. I'm not scared."

His brothers laughed. "*Little* Jamie! The *big hero*!" they shouted, and, catching hold of him, rolled him on the ground in a rough and tumble – six against one – until their father stopped them.

When Jamie got to his feet, he stuck his chin in the air. "I could have beaten the lot of you!" he said. "But I am saving my strength – for Master Stoorworm!"

That night Jamie lay quietly in his bed. He had made his plans. He was going to fight Master Stoorworm.

As soon as everyone else was fast asleep, he crept outside, mounted his father's horse and galloped off. The moon was full, and the sky starry bright, so Jamie easily found the path that led to the seashore.

When he came to a small, one-roomed cottage, he jumped off the horse, tethered him to the gate post and walked in at the door. Jamie's old granny lay in bed snoring, the peat fire was banked up and on the floor, beside it, stood an iron pot. Jamie bent over, picked up a glowing peat from the fire, placed it in the pot, and crept out as softly as he came. His granny heard nothing.

Only the grey cat at the bottom of her bed looked up and stretched himself.

15

King Harald's boat was ready, mast up and afloat in the shallow water, with the boatman sitting in it, swinging his arms across his chest to warm himself.

Jamie called out, "It's a rare nippy morning! Why don't you take a run on the shore and warm yourself?"

"Leave the boat? I wouldn't dare!" the boatman called back. "The chief steward would have me beaten black and blue if anything happened to the king's boat today!"

Jamie put down the iron pot and began poking around in a rock pool, as if he were collecting shellfish. Suddenly he jumped up and yelled out: "Gold! Gold! Yes! It's bright as the sun! It must be gold!"

This was too much for the boatman. In less than a minute he was out of the boat, across the sands and down on his knees by the rock pool, looking for gold.

And Jamie? He picked up the pot with the live peat in it, walked lightly across the sands, untied the boat rope, jumped aboard, grabbed hold of an oar and pushed off.

By the time the boatman looked up, Jamie was out at sea, with sail up and flying. The boatman was furious. He waved his arms and yelled the angriest, rudest words he could think of. But there was nothing he could do.

When King Harald, his chief steward, the princess and their servants arrived, they too were furious. And when a whole crowd of curious folk, including Jamie's family, arrived, they were not pleased either. But what could they do? Nothing but wait and watch.

Meanwhile Jamie pointed the small boat towards Master Stoorworm's mountainous head and sailed on. When he came close, he jammed the boat up against the monster's mouth, pulled in the oars and rested.

The sun, round and red, rose slowly above a distant valley. Its bright rays struck Master Stoorworm's two big eyes, and he woke. His wide mouth stretched open, and he began the first of the seven yawns, that he yawned each morning before eating breakfast.

Now, as Master Stoorworm breathed in, a flood of sea water swept into his mouth and down his throat – and the boat and Jamie were sucked in with it.

On and on, faster and faster, the boat was swept down and along the monster's throat, which was softly lit, here and there, by a silvery phosphorescent light.

20

At last the water became shallower
and the boat was grounded. Jamie lifted
the iron pot, jumped out of the boat and
ran on until he came to the monster's
liver. He pulled a knife out of his pocket,
cut a hole in the oily
liver and stuffed
the glowing peat
into the hole.
He blew and
blew until he
thought his lips
would crack.
But, in the end, the
peat burst into flame, the
oil in the liver hissed and sputtered, there
was a flash, and the liver was ablaze.

Jamie ran back to the boat, fast as he
could lift his feet. He jumped in and held
tight. He was only just in time.

When Master Stoorworm felt the fierce heat of the fire inside him, he twisted and turned and threshed about with such violence that he threw up. The entire contents of the monster's enormous stomach came torrenting up his throat,  caught hold of the boat, swept it along and along, up and out of his mouth, across the sea, till it landed, high and dry, on a sand dune.

No one took any notice of Jamie! The king and everyone who had come to watch, and that included Jamie's granny and the grey cat who had been woken by the commotion, were all running off to the top of the nearest hill.

22

Jamie was out of the boat in a moment and soon chasing after them trying to escape the huge waves that were thundering ashore as Master Stoorworm violently twisted and turned.

By now the monster was more to be pitied than feared. Black clouds of smoke were belching out of his mouth and nostrils as the fire inside him grew fiercer. He tossed to and fro. He flung out his forked tongue and stretched it, up and up, towards the cool sky. He tossed his head and his tongue fell down so hard and fast it made a huge dent in the earth, and the sea rushed in. And that dent became the crooked straits which now separate Denmark from Norway and Sweden.

Master Stoorwom drew in his tongue and this time flung his head, up and up, towards the cool sky. He tossed his head, and down it came so hard and fast that some of his teeth fell out and landed in the sea. And they became the scattered islands that are now known as the Orkney Isles.

Again his head rose up, he tossed it, and when it came down, a lot more teeth fell out. And they became the Shetland Isles.

A third time the head rose up, and when it came down, the rest of his teeth fell out. And they became the Faroe Isles.

After that Master Stoorworm coiled himself, round and round, into a great lump, and he died. And this lump became Iceland, and the fire which Jamie lit with the burning peat still burns beneath that land. Even today, there are mountains in Iceland which throw out fire.

When everyone was absolutely certain Master Stoorworm was dead, King Harald could scarcely contain himself. He threw his arms round Jamie and called him his son, and took off his royal cloak and put it on Jamie, and gave him the precious sword, Sicker Snapper. And then the king took hold of the princess's hand and put it in Jamie's hand.

So then there was a wedding – and such a wedding! The feasting and dancing lasted for nine whole weeks. Everyone was so happy because Master Stoorworm was dead and now they could live in peace. And everyone, Jamie's brothers included, agreed that Jamie was their champion and – *a big hero!*

*A Scandinavian tale
told in the Orkney Isles*

THE UNICORN

The Unicorn is a beautiful and mysterious beast who always walks alone. He is rarely seen. But once – and *only* once – the Unicorn did come among the other animals. And that one and only time he shared with them his strange and magical powers.

Far, far away there was a wood, and under the shady trees there was a pool of fresh water. It was the animals' pool, where they all came to drink.

Now for months there had been no rain and the sun had shone, hot and fierce. The streams and rivers dried up. The grass turned yellowy-brown. Even the weeds frizzled up and dried. But the animals' pool, under the shady trees, stayed full to the brim. It never failed. And so the animals had enough water to drink.

Until, one day, a serpent came slithering out of a cave. He moved fast across the dry grass, into the wood and straight towards the animals' pool. When

he reached the water's edge, he slowly raised his head and, swaying from side to side, stretched over the pool and spurted out a flood of deadly poison. It floated across the surface like oil, covering the whole of the pool. Then the serpent moved off, fast as he came, back to his cave.

And why did the serpent do this? Because he was wicked. Because he felt like it. And because he cared for no one but himself. That was why.

At their usual times, the animals sauntered along in ones or twos, or friendly little groups towards the pool. But as soon as they reached the water's edge, they smelt the poison and saw it floating on the surface, and they knew that if they swallowed it, they would die.

Some animals were so upset they moaned quietly. Others yelped and roared their anger. Not one turned back and left.

By evening there was a huge crowd round the pool. Animals who were definitely *not* good friends and who *never* drank together stood side by side: the lion, the buffalo and the antelope, the wolf, the camel, the donkey and the sheep…and many more besides.

Night came, the moon rose in the sky, and still more animals came. From time to time, some would call out, and then others would add their voices to the loud, mournful cry. Each time the cry grew louder. Was there no one who could help them?

The Unicorn, the beautiful one who walks alone, was far off, but at last he heard the animals' cry. He listened and understood. He kicked up his hoofs and came trotting, slowly at first, but steadily gaining speed until he was galloping faster than the wind.

As he approached the wood he slowed down, and then, stepping softly, he wound his way in and out among the trees. He saw the animals gathered round the pool. He smelt the poison. Then he knew everything.

The Unicorn knelt beside the pool, lowered his head and dipped his long pointed horn into the water, deeper and deeper, until it was completely covered. He waited a moment and then slowly lifted his horn out of the water. He stood up. His magical horn had done its work. The poison was gone. The water was fresh and pure again.

Without pushing, nudging or quarrelling of any kind, the animals lowered their heads and drank. When their thirst was quenched and their strength returned, they all called out, with one voice, their thanks to the Unicorn.

But he was not there. He had left while they were drinking. His work was done. He needed no one. He was the Unicorn who walks alone.

A European tale

THE KING WHO WANTED TO TOUCH THE MOON

Long ago there lived a king who always had to have his own way. Everyone had to do exactly what he said. Immediately. No talk, no arguing.

Well, one night this king looked out
of the window and saw the silvery moon
riding high in the sky
and, there and
then, he wanted
to reach out
and touch it.
But even he
couldn't do
that. So he
thought about
it, and he
thought about it.
Night and day he

thought about it. And at last he worked
out a way of touching the moon. He
would have a tall, tall tower built that
reached to the sky, and then, when he had
climbed to the top, he would be able to
touch the moon.

So the king sent for the royal carpenter and ordered him to build the tower.

The carpenter shook his head. "A tower so tall that it reaches right to the moon? Your majesty, it is not possible. It can't be done."

"Can't?" shouted the king. "No such word as can't in this kingdom. Come back tomorrow morning, first thing, and tell me exactly how you are going to build my tower."

That night the carpenter did some hard thinking, and in the end worked out a way of building a tall tower.

The next morning he went to the king and said, "Your majesty, the way to build the tower is to pile up lots of strong wooden chests, one on top of the other, hundreds and thousands of them, until they reach to the sky."

Now the king liked this idea. So he ordered his subjects to search their homes and bring all their strong chests to the palace. Immediately. And if anyone refused? Well, there was plenty of room in the royal prisons for them.

So, of course, the people brought their chests and gave them to the king. And there were all kinds of chests – big and small, carved, polished, painted and plain.

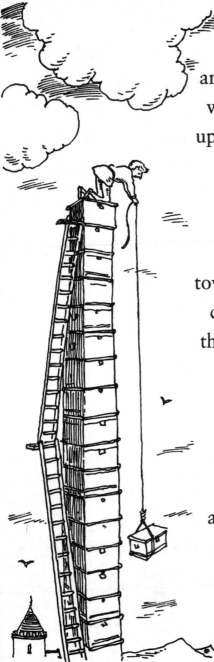

Then the carpenter and his assistant set to work. They laid chest upon chest, one on top of the other, up and up, and before long, outside the palace, there stood a tall tower. But when all the chests had been used, the tower did not even reach to the clouds. The king said to the carpenter, "Make some more chests!" So wood was found and the carpenter and his assistants sawed and hammered and made more chests.

Then they added
these to the tower,
laying chest upon
chest, one on top
of the other, up
and up. But when
all the chests had been
used, the tower only reached to the
clouds. The king said to the carpenter,
"Make some more chests!"

"There is no more wood, your majesty,"
said the carpenter.

"Then cut down all the trees and get
some wood," ordered the king.

The carpenter shook his head. "*All* the
trees!" he said. "Oh no, we can't do that—"

"Did I hear you say 'can't'? Have you
forgotten that there is no such word as can't
in this kingdom?" said the king. "Go and
cut down *all* the trees. Immediately."

So then all the trees in the kingdom were chopped down – the great ancient trees and the slender saplings, the fruit trees and the nut trees and the flowering trees – all were cut down and sawn into planks and made into chests. More and more chests. And

the chests were laid one on top of the other. Up and up. And when all the chests had been used, the tower reached beyond the clouds and up into the sky.

The king looked at the tower and he was pleased. He said, "The time has come for me to climb my tall, tall tower and touch the moon."

He began to climb, up and up and up, until at last he stood at the top of his tall, tall tower. He looked up and he stretched out both his arms, but he could not quite reach to the moon. He stood on the very tips of his toes and stretched some more. He was so very close. He could almost touch the moon. But not quite.

He shouted down, "Bring up another chest! Just one! That will be enough!"

The carpenter looked around. There were no chests left. No wood left. And not a single tree in all the land.

So he called out, "Your majesty, there are *no more chests*!"

The king shouted back, "THEN TAKE ONE OUT FROM THE BOTTOM AND BRING THAT UP HERE!"

The carpenter was astonished. He couldn't take a chest out from the bottom of the pile. Well, could he? Surely, the king was not serious. Then he heard the king shouting again.

"DIDN'T YOU HEAR ME? TAKE ONE OUT FROM THE BOTTOM! IMMEDIATELY!"

The carpenter raised his eyebrows, shrugged his shoulders and then did as he was told. He pulled a chest out from the bottom of the pile.

And you can imagine what happened next. The whole tall tower came tumbling down, king, chests and all. So that was the end of the king who always had to have his own way and who wanted, above everything else, to touch the moon.

A Caribbean tale told
in the Dominican Republic

THE GIANT SEA SERPENT

A Scandinavian Tale told in the Orkney Isles

Some Scandinavian tales tell of a gigantic serpent that lies at the bottom of the sea, curled right around the earth. Master Stoorworm, in *The Giant Sea Serpent* story collected in the Orkney Isles, seems rather like this serpent – 'worm' being the old name for one.

Although the Orkney and Shetland Isles are now part of Scotland, they have a heritage of stories from their Scandinavian past. Vikings, from Norway, settled on these islands and for about six hundred years they belonged to the King of Norway. They were given to Scotland in 1472.

When Jamie triumphs over the Stoorworm, he relies on his own cleverness and courage. He is much smaller than the serpent, but by allowing himself to be swallowed, he can reach the creature's weak spot and set it alight. In his death throes, the giant Stoorworm creates various countries that belonged to the Vikings, at one time or another. He is even given as the reason why there are hot springs and volcanoes in Iceland!

46

THE UNICORN

A European Tale

Two thousand years ago, a Greek doctor wrote that, in India, there were wild asses who had one pointed horn. A cup made from it would protect the drinker from poison. Some Europeans believed this was true.

The Unicorn began its written life in a European bestiary – a book of facts and fables about real and imaginary animals. As in the story, the unicorn was always thought to be a solitary and powerful animal.

THE KING WHO WANTED TO TOUCH THE MOON

A Caribbean Tale told in the Dominican Republic

The King Who Wanted to Touch the Moon is about a dictator who thinks he can have *anything* he wants. In the end it is his own stupidity and selfishness that brings him down to earth with a bump!

Like many stories of the Caribbean islands, this Dominican one was brought by African slaves. In a version collected in Africa, the king has a bamboo tower built, in order to reach the treasure in the sky.

47

MAGICAL TALES
from
AROUND THE WORLD

Retold by Margaret Mayo ✳ *Illustrated by Peter Bailey*

Orchard Myths are available from all good bookshops,
or can be ordered direct from the publisher:
Orchard Books, PO BOX 29, Douglas IM99 1BQ
Credit card orders please telephone 01624 836000
or fax 01624 837033
or e-mail: bookshop@enterprise.net for details.

To order please quote title, author and ISBN
and your full name and address.
Cheques and postal orders should be
made payable to 'Bookpost plc'.
Postage and packing is FREE within the UK
(overseas customers should add £1.00 per book).

Prices and availability are subject to change.